EDEN *miniatures*

EDEN *miniatures*

Dimensions
Heart
The Snowflake Collector
The Ice King
The Planet Walk
The Tape
Istanbul
Sedartis
Encounters
The Bournemouth & Boscombe Trilogy
Insomnia
Euphoria

THE BOURNEMOUTH & BOSCOMBE TRILOGY

Optimist

The Bournemouth &
Boscombe Trilogy

I

Pyromania

It was a particularly pointless but spectacular crime that shook the town, the nation, the world.

It could not be explained, even though the Earnest Psychologist tried, on TV, to find reason for it, or if not reason, then at least rhyme. It could not be put to use, even though the Angry Prophet admonished the people for failing to see its hidden purpose; and it could not, so it seemed—oh could it ever?—be forgiven.

The Sacred Sage counselled thus, but the offence was so severe, the laceration so visceral, and the shock so unshakeable that the hand of mercy may not extend for millennia. As for the Messenger? The furious rabble killed her on the spot.

George had recently moved to the area, and he was in no way unusual, other than in the ways that everyone is a bit, especially when puberty all of a sudden gives way to sullen teenage anguish.

George's anguish was no different to most, so most would have said, but he alone had to bear it, and he knew that nobody knew what it was. Nor did he care. Nor did he think about it or dwell on its nature. He felt an ache of malcontent with the world that was heavy and sad, and he didn't have words to talk about it, nor did he have friends who would have responded in terms of pure friendship if he had ever articulated it.

The Earnest Psychologist, in retrospect, tried to reason that the breakup of his parents two years prior would have been an incision of trauma and separation in his life. The Angry Prophet berated the people: your passive aggression, your smug disengagement, your unbearable peace! Someone needed to come and infuriate you! Shake you! His pain is now yours. Own his pain! And turn it on the system that pains *you!*

The Sacred Sage knew not of pain or system, but he knew of love. 'Love this boy, he is your son,' he said, as they shouted him down. 'The world you are part of—that you are a creation and at the same time creators of—is the world that has all of you in it and all that you hold dear, and it has also him in it, and all that you despise; if you despise him, you despise part of you: the hatred that pains you is the hatred for the part of you that you don't want to know. Love him like your son; more than your son! Love him and forgive him: extend the hand of friendship to him and say these words: "you are forgiven."'

But George was not forgiven. They cried, 'he has not atoned, and he has not shown remorse, he has not begged for our forgiveness, on his knees, as he must, since the horrendousness of his deed has no bounds.' The Sacred Sage sighed.

George had been wandering along the beach that he had recently moved to, with his father, a spruce man called Mark. Mark was a good dad to George, and he loved his son in an uncomplicated way that as far as he knew and was able to tell made sense and sufficed. It was not an ungenerous love, it was genuine. Real. George had no reason to doubt that his dad loved him, and his dad was far from his mind.

On his mind was nothing specific as he ambled, listlessly, on the promenade from his new flat—he did not think of it yet as his home; events he himself was about to unleash were to make sure that he never would—by Boscombe Pier towards Bournemouth town. He wasn't thinking of his friends (he had one or two), or his class mates (he was mostly indifferent to them), nor was he thinking of any girl.

Sometimes he thought of a girl; there was one in his class who was undeniably pretty, and sassy too, and whose lips curled up by the edge of her mouth when she smiled, which he thought was attractive, and her name was Sarah, which reminded him of his aunt, who was also called Sarah, but he was not thinking of his aunt either that evening, making his way slowly towards Bournemouth.

He wasn't thinking of homework, nor of any sports team he may or may not have had a passing interest in, and he wasn't thinking of a nondescript future. Nor was he thinking there was no future, or that the future would be nondescript. (As it turned out, the future for George would be highly specific.)

He was moving at the languid pace of a lanky youth westwards, and he was going to meet up with some mates. This thought, such as it was, neither uneased nor excited him: it was one of those things that you did. So George's head was not filled with anything in particular at this time: he was neither angry nor sad, not lonely nor elated. He hadn't had anything to drink at this point, and he had not taken any drugs either. The Earnest Psychologist found this hardest to deal with in retrospect: there was no trigger, no immediate cause. Not now, and not in the hours and days that followed. The Angry Prophet disagreed: the cause was all around! The cause was there right in front of everyone: just look and you see it, open your eyes!

The Sacred Sage knew not of any cause or what causes might be 'good' or 'sufficient' or 'real'; he spake unto them: 'have done with fear and loathing and hatred and cause. Love

him as if he had given or needed no cause.'
They yelled at him chants of shame and
abuse.

What caught George's eye and his attention,
and filled his head with a leftfield thought—
one that seemed to come out of nowhere
and should have fleeted through his mind
without trace, but didn't: it lodged itself
there and nested, and laid its eggs and sat
on them, warm and soft and heavy, till these
thought-eggs hatched, and they were not
quiet or timid, but loud and vigorous and
demanding to be fed with action—what
ignited the spark of mischievous unrest that
would have to (there already was no escape)
yield onto abject disaster, but also glorious
ecstasy, if but for one moment – what was
on his mind were the beach huts.

To his left, the sand, brought here from
elsewhere to cover the shingles; beyond the
sand, the sea, unceasing in its undulation.
Wave upon wave, ripples upon ripples. The
constant sound of undramatic motion.

To his right, the beach huts. All locked up,
this time of day, bar two or three: exceptions.
They were modest huts, almost sheds, really,
perhaps four feet wide and six feet tall, barely
tall enough for a grown man to stand up
in. George was no grown man, and at 5'7"
he was unlikely to turn into a giant among
them. He had a slim and slender stature.

The huts all carried numbers. Here, they
were in the low to mid-hundreds. They lined
up one by one, not in clusters but in single
file segments. Sometimes a dozen, sometimes
two. They seemed of an ilk, though

occasionally George walked past some newer models, ones with roll-down shutters, or wooden roofs, instead of the black rough material most were covered with. They were not deep, maybe another five or six feet. Inside, there was room to stow away some deckchairs, some wind breaker thing or some chairs and a parasol. Mostly it was too windy for parasols here.

At this time in the early evening, when the sun is beginning its hesitant descent, not over the sea but behind the slightly elevated land, most people have either not been here or they've already left. Only now and then do you walk past someone putting away the things they've been using during the day, or reading a few more pages in their book, or sitting with two or three friends in chairs outside the open hut, drinking cider.

Many, though by no means all, of the huts have a little gas stove, with only two rings:

enough to heat up a kettle or a tin of baked beans. The huts all sit off the ground on stout ledges made of brick, and they are very close to each other, nearly touching, but not quite, unless there's an actual gap, in which case it's mostly several huts wide and there for a reason: a public convenience or a small ice cream parlour, or some similar unflattering, utilitarian structure.

Sometimes there is a long gap with no huts for a few dozen or a few hundred yards, and then they start up again. There is nothing strange or exceptional about these beach huts, except perhaps their very existence. It is a little miracle of quaintness in an otherwise strident world. They are so small, these huts, so modest, so impractical, in a way, and they're not even directly on the beach, they're on the other side of the promenade: everyone can partake of them, the people sitting outside them watching the people go by, and the people going by watching the people sitting outside them. They are not private. There is nothing exclusive about them, let alone glamorous. Some have whimsical, punning names: "Mad Hutter," for instance, or "Seas The Day." Inside the odd one, with its wooden shutters open, you spot little signs or postcards that say things like: "O I do like to be beside the seaside," or "A day at the sea is good for the soul."

They can't be argued with, these huts, they are part of the seafront, like seagulls and groins and the piers and the surfers and the signs listing all the things you can't do, now that you're here.

George knew these huts, of course, he'd walked past them innumerable times: he was hardly surprised by their presence. Nor was he annoyed. Nor was he thrilled. Or even delighted. Yet into his mind slipped a thought that put a smile on his face, that was almost a grin. How easy it would be to set them on fire. All it took, he immediately recognised while walking by, was for a small incendiary device to be placed in the gap made by the pedestal each sat on, and within seconds the thing could be ablaze. What's more—and this thought followed on directly from the first—no sooner would one have caught fire, than the two next to it would do too.

In fact, and George who had a visual brain imagined this as a diagram straight away, you only had to light numbers 2, 5, 8 and 11 in any row of twelve to be sure they would all go up in flames almost simultaneously:

1 - 2 - 3 - 4 - 5 - 6 - 7 - 8 - 9 - 10 - 11 - 12
o - √ - o - o - √ - o - o - √ - o - o - √ - o

That's one in three, George thought, and the smile on his face broadened; and his eyes, dulled by the ordinariness of his life thus far, lit up, just a little.

George knew nothing about incendiary devices. What he noticed, however, over the next three or four days, as he walked past these huts during the daytime, up and down the beach in both directions from his flat near Boscombe Pier, was that not all, but many of them must have, tucked away inside them, a bottle of Calor or similar gas, used to fuel the mini-stoves.

This would make his task—and that it had already turned into a task, of this he felt pretty certain—so much easier. It also prescribed his window of opportunity. The bottles, he reasoned, would be unlikely to be there, or come into much use, out of or towards the end of the season. And the season was not yet in swing. It was early June, the sea temperature at around twelve degrees Celsius was not yet attractive to casual bathers (even if some hardy swimmers could always be spotted of a late afternoon or early evening dipping themselves into the water), and so it would make sense, he believed, to strike at a significant-enough moment, soon.

George's one or two friends at school were not the kind you could make accomplices in what he knew was not going to be an easy undertaking, and also not one designed to make him popular with his relatively new neighbours or the holidaymakers who rented the huts for the summer or part thereof. He had no confidant either. The time frame he had just set himself was clearly too short to acquire one too, and so he would have to rely on his own resources and relish the moment, when it came, most likely on his own. This did not make George sad, he was used to doing things on his own.

Except, there was a boy at school who liked
and watched him more than he knew.
Whether it was a teenage crush, or simple
idolisation of an older, cooler, more worldly
youth, or whether it was something else,
neither George, nor the boy, nor their
parents, nor the Earnest Psychologist,
would ever be able to tell with any degree
of certainty, or authority, even though the
Earnest Psychologist tried.

The boy's name was Andy, and he
was two years younger than George,
just turned thirteen. He'd been aware of
George for a good few weeks now, ever since
George had arrived at school, as it happened,
and he'd known, instinctively, that there was
something special, something noteworthy,
something edgy and therefore interesting
about him. He half expected to find that
George owned a snake or collected spiders
or kept a diary in Esperanto, none of which
George did. Still, Andy's young, distant

assessment of George's character was not altogether wide of the mark.

Little Andy—he was remarkably short and remarkably nimble on his feet, and swift with his hands—surprised George just as he was looking up small detonators on the school computer. George used the school computer for doing his research because he reasoned that on a computer used by teenagers of all predilections there were bound to appear search terms associated with blowing up stuff, without attracting the immediate attention of MI5.

'What are you doing?' Andy asked, in his forthright, unawkward manner that stood in such contrast to his shy demeanour. George looked up (only a little up: Andy standing virtually came face to face with George sitting) and fixed his eyes straight into Andy's:

'I'm going to make some beach huts go bang.'

'Really?'

'Yes.'

'How?'

'I'm just finding out.'

'Which ones?'

'Ideally: all of them.'

'Wow.'

'Yep.'

'All of them?'

'Can you imagine?'

'You'd see that for …miles.'

'Exactly.'

'When?'

'Summer Solstice.'

'Summer Solstice?'

'Summer Solstice.'

Andy was already a conspirator. He didn't know it yet, the Judge, on the counsel of another, quite equally earnest, psychologist, with appalled leniency in her eyes, would

later abnegate it, but Andy knew, and
George knew, they were now in this
together.

    'That's soon, isn't it?'
    'It's in three weeks.'
    'Wow.'
    'Yup.'
    'Better get a move on then.'

George shut the computer and stood up,
now in his moderate but lanky length
towering over little Andy. He ruffled
his hair. Andy felt a shudder of delight
charge through his young body. The fear
of the forbidden, paired with a ripple of
inexplicable lust.

What little George needed to know about incendiary devices, he learnt very quickly; and Andy turned out to be an ideal accomplice. While George was methodical, wily and determined, Andy was swift, small and silent, and quite original in his thinking.

The biggest challenge, George surmised, would be to procure a large number of detonators and wiring, without raising suspicion, let alone alarm. But in actual fact, this proved a lot easier than he had anticipated: relying mostly on the Calor gas bottles for the 'bang', George reckoned that with a few very ordinary household items and some basic physics he could most likely create simultaneous sparks, and if he could do that, he could ignite simultaneous boxes of matches and some firelighters or sponges doused in white spirit or petrol, and if he could do that, he could not, perhaps, cause simultaneous bangs, but the random series that would result in different huts exploding at slightly different times would lend the spectacle its own satisfying symphonic quality.

Conscious of the 'one chance to get this right' aspect to his endeavour, combined with a patent inability to do a test run, even on a model or an isolated, remote specimen, George felt there was a lot at stake and a lot that could go wrong. He confided this worry, such as it was, in passing to Andy. Andy was unperturbed:

'Yeah you can run a test.'

'Where would I run a test?'

'There are beach huts on every other beach in the country: just go to a beach and do just the one, nobody will think it's a test, they'll just think: fuck, the hut blew up. Bum*mer.*'

That made sense. It would be no more difficult than travelling to another beach, remote enough so as not to draw attention to Boscombe and Bournemouth and close enough so as not to take more than an hour's travel or so, and a field test could be run on just one, perhaps slightly isolated beach hut that looked like it might recently have been in use and that fulfilled the principal criteria set by his actual target huts for reference.

'Brighton.' Andy did not need to think about this.

'Brighton is miles away. And it's extremely busy.'

'Exactly. It's miles away, and nobody would think anybody from Bournemouth would be stupid enough to go there just to blow up a beach hut. Plus there are any number of people off their heads enough there to set fire to one of their huts by accident.'

The reasoning was flawless. It was risky, George thought, but on balance, and thinking about it a bit further, longer and more thoroughly, not as risky, most likely, as going to a remote beach where two teenagers, one lanky and tall, the other tiny and cute, would be instantly memorable. In Brighton, nobody would bat an eyelid. All they had to do was go there, find the right hut, maybe somewhat to the end of the beach, and run their test without getting caught. It would be like a rehearsal. It would be indispensable, George suddenly realised. Of course they had to do a test.

Now the question was: how to stay away overnight without raising eyebrows...

'We go and visit my uncle, Edward,' Andy suggested.

'Great, where does he live?'

'In London, of course.'

'Of course.'

George told his dad, Andy his mother; they would spend a weekend in London with Uncle Edward. Uncle Edward was asked and readily agreed, he was looking forward to seeing them.

Once in London, they would simply go out, as you do of a Saturday night, and return very late or early next morning. Uncle Edward would not ask them where they had been, or if he did, he would do so in the way uncles do: all right boys, have you had a good time last night? Yeah. Where did you go? Oh we went out. Great. Help yourselves to juice in the fridge and whatever there is to eat.

There wouldn't be much to eat in the fridge, and the juice would be something like 'Açaí Berry' or 'Radiant Beetroot', but no further questions would be asked. The thought that the boys might have taken a train down to Brighton would not occur to Uncle Edward,

and if it did, he'd think that was a splendid
idea. But they wouldn't tell him, just in case
by some freakish coincidence the 'news' of
a beach hut in Brighton having blown up
might reach London. They thought that
was extremely unlikely, it would be more
likely—though still wildly improbable—to
reach Bournemouth, in a 'typical: someone
in Brighton blew up their hut...' kind of way.

Time was tight, but Uncle Edward
confirmed he'd be around the following
weekend; and the weather, as if to order, was
gorgeous.

The hut made the front page of the *Argos*. That in itself, George felt, was quite satisfying. He and Andy were already back in Bournemouth by the time they found out, online, that their test had become a local news item in Brighton & Hove.

It nearly didn't. When they got to Brighton, exactly as planned and with no eyebrows raised from anyone, via Uncle Edward's in London, they found to their dismay that Brighton beach huts in the main were bigger, fatter and squatter than those on Boscombe Beach and, more to the point, they mostly sat flat on the ground.

George's approach had been—and to all intents and purposes still was—to plant a tiny charge of homemade explosive under each third hut and, considering the average distance at which they are spaced, hook three charges up to one kitchen timer. Preassembled and primed, it would then be possible for two people to, comparatively swiftly, place the devices in batches of three, in a relay sequence.

Bearing in mind the overall distance to be covered, any obstacles on the way, and the obvious need to remain inconspicuous, they had, he estimated, a window of opportunity lasting approximately three hours. If one person was able to plant one set every two minutes, then, allowing for a margin of error of ten minutes per hour, the two of them would be able to plant fifty sets an hour, which would cover 450 huts. Times three made roughly 1350. That, George thought, was not quite enough. He had been hoping for about twice as many. But Andy remained unperturbed: 'You're not thinking of the wind.'

That was true, George had not been thinking of the wind. Could he think of the wind?

'We don't know what the wind will be doing on Midsummer Night.'

'It always does something, and it normally comes in from about there.'

Andy was standing on Brighton Beach, facing the water and pointing vaguely to his right. What was true of Brighton was also true of Bournemouth and of most of the English South Coast. The wind, mostly, came vaguely from the right.

That made a big difference. As George knew—although he had never expressed it and didn't do so now—in the face of uncertainty, likelihood is your friend. And in all likelihood the wind on Summer Solstice Night would do on Bournemouth and Boscombe Beaches exactly what it normally does: come in vaguely from the right, more or less the south west.

This could double capacity at a stroke. Maybe not quite double. For practical reasons, the individual devices within each set could not be spaced further than two huts apart, not least because George and Andy had by now started assembling them. But the sets themselves: they could be spaced out a bit. Perhaps as much as three huts apart. So George's diagram in his mind now looked more like this:

1	2	3	4	5	6	7	8	9	10	11	12	13	14	15	16	17	18	19	20	21
o	√	o	o	√	o	o	√	o	x	x	x	o	√	o	o	√	o	o	√	o

Which meant one set of three could actually cover a dozen huts. A hundred and fifty sets would now light up 1,800 of them. That was a pleasing number, George thought, and Andy thought so too:

'It's pleasing,' Andy said. It sounded slightly odd, coming from a teenager barely

the size of a twelve year old, but it was true.
It was pleasing.

The project of getting hold of a hundred
and fifty kitchen timers had started almost
immediately, but the trip to Brighton, via
London, proved instrumental, because there
are only so many kitchen timers you can
nick in and around Bournemouth before
somebody starts thinking that's odd. The
trip to Brighton via London though took
in numerous household and hardware
stores, DIY centres and ordinary larger
scale supermarkets, in none of which digital
kitchen timers were considered high enough
value items to be individually tagged, with
maybe one or two exceptions of the more
'designer' variety.

George and Andy eschewed those and
bagged the smallest and cheapest they could
find, and before long their little suitcases

were filling up with timers of every type and description.

Uncle Edward remained oblivious to all this, as he was not the kind of grown-up to snoop into teenagers' bags, or any of his house guests' for that matter, of whom he had many. He wished them a good night out on the Saturday, when he was going to the theatre and dinner with a friend, and they headed down to Brighton.

As previously agreed, they did not tell Uncle Edward they were taking a train down to Brighton, so as far as he was concerned, they were just heading into town. They did not specifically tell him that's what they were doing either, because it went against George's grain to lie to his uncle, whom, after all, he liked very much.

Following what looked like a potentially fatal setback, owing to the 'wrong' beach hut design being prevalent on this part of the coast, the two boys—who here, among the curious mix of the youthful laid-back, the middle aged gay and the residual resident retired looked oddly at home—on their stroll happened upon a hut that seemed, and turned out, just about perfect: part of a group that looked a little older than the others, it sat on a low but accessible base, it was in good but not pristine condition, and its location, towards the end of the beach, made it, if not exactly isolated, then still comparatively quiet.

With the temperature mild, and just a faint breeze wafting in from, vaguely, the right, and the hour approaching midnight now, there were people milling about, but not too many and, as predicted and hoped, none of them paid any attention to the odd young couple among them. At this point, poised and calm, they didn't look like juvenile arsonists, at least no more than juveniles do without meaning to anyway. They looked like any teenagers, one tall and languid, the other minuscule and mercurial, who probably should be heading home about now, and who might be doing just that, albeit slowly.

The deed itself was done in seconds and, within the specified minutes of deliberately 'programmed' delay, resulted in a resounding success.

The display on the night was magnificent: the dreadful beauty of destruction. Summer Solstice in Bournemouth and Boscombe would never be the same again. Some people, idiotically, would refer to it later as the 'Midsummer Massacre'. It was, of course, nothing of the sort. But it was violent, catastrophic. And exceptionally elegant too.

The people in Totland, on the Isle of Wight, probably had the best view, apart perhaps from some revellers who had gone down to the Needles and stayed there till sunrise.

George and Andy never gave a name to what they did, and by no stretch of the imagination could it truthfully be described as a 'massacre', either by intention or by effect. That it therefore, somewhat clumsily and by the uncomfortable default that envelops events which happen too quickly and then linger, became known as the Solstice Spectacle, is largely attributable to a couple of unassuming and in most senses of the word pretty average men in their thirties, Stefano and Paul, one Italian, the other English, who had decided to spend the afternoon on Studland Beach and—having previously been oblivious to its naturist stretch—found themselves teased out of their swimwear for the first time in a more or less public place by sheer opportunity.

They had brought along a picnic hamper and two bottles of Verdicchio (Stefano had insisted it not be Pinot Grigio, for once!) and gone through said bottles with unsurprising ease by the time it got dark. After that, they felt comfortably relaxed, but also just a tad horny, and not wanting to risk making a nuisance of themselves or incurring the wrath of other naturists, they withdrew a bit behind some dunes and the long grass, where they no more than lay in each other's arms and maybe fondled each other a bit before, in the unusually warm air of the night—even for a Midsummer Night on an English beach—they dozed off.

They woke up again at what must have been some time after midnight, maybe close to one, and the alcohol having eased off but not so much their libido, Stefano remembered that he may just have a tiny bit of M left in his backpack, from a session he had been to with a couple of guys a few months earlier, which had been really rather enjoyable.

This proved to be the case, and although the little sachet he'd pushed down one of the outside pockets of the backpack at the time on parting and more or less forgotten about contained just enough for maybe twice two shortish lines, that was certainly enough to give them a pretty good time for the next couple of hours or so.

Stefano was in a blissful place looking out
over the expanse of the sea upside down on
the sandy slope towards the beach with Paul
over him and inside him, the two of them
so into each other, so in synch, so absorbed
in their rhythm that nothing, nothing else
mattered, that everything, everything was
good and warm and I-am-you-and-you-are-
me, and the way they were together they
both got to the point where soon—but
please not just yet!—they both would erupt;
and they built up to it and they moaned and
groaned and called each other's names and
oh yeah and oh god and *dio mio* and *not yet!*
and I want to cum, and me too and yeah
do it and yeah do it and just as they did—
Stefano a fraction sooner, which tipped
Paul now over the edge too—just at that
moment the sky and the beach and the sea lit
up and their orgasms lasted and lasted and
their happiness and their joy and their union
was complete and a chain of lights adorned

the coast, in explosion after explosion,
like gorgeous fire crackers in the distance,
and blue flashes sparked and yellow flames
danced and thick smoke rose in the purple
red orange skies and both of them lost their
minds for minutes and maybe for hours but
for these moments they were it all and it all
was they and that was the universe and the
universe was wonderful and one.

There were maybe two dozen or so other
nude people who had elected or ended
up spending the night on the beach and
none of them had really been particularly
aware of these two. Sure, if those who had
settled in closest had kept quiet and still for
a while they would probably have heard,
faint in the distance, the unmistakable
noises of two people getting high on a
recreational substance and on each other,
but nobody did, because they had their own
conversations, one small group even had
their guitars, some had their whispers and

others their quieter unions to celebrate, and so nobody had minded or noted the glorious coming together of Stefano and Paul.

But now everybody was on their feet, by the water, watching the spectacle unfolding on Bournemouth and Boscombe Beaches, all the way from Sandbanks to Christchurch; it was awesome in every original sense of the word: awe-inspiring and profound. Stefano, still high as a kite, and like the others on the beach largely naked—some, perhaps, had put on a shirt or wrapped a shawl round their shoulders—was in a Heaven all of his own, exclaiming in Italian, '*mamma mia! che bello! dio mio! che spettacolo! che spettacolo! che spettacolo*' and Paul, equally high but less Mediterranean in his expression, kept hugging him and smiling and laughing and smiling and kissing him and then they just held hands and stood there, naked as the universe had made them, among the others

who stood there naked and amazed and
awed.

And so it came to be that by far the most
vivid, most famous, most watched and most
liked, most discussed, also, most shared and
most, in its own peculiar way, cherished
video of the most horrific devastation ever
unleashed on the English Seaside was also,
and looked and felt and sounded and would
be experienced for decades by people the
world over as, a fantastic, poetic, ecstatic
celebration of humans just as they are, as
they are when in love.

Morning crept up on Boscombe Beach like a girl, home late from a party: a little tousled, a little ablush; in the small hours, with a hazy memory at best of what had happened the night before.

Andy and George had taken a boat from the boat house at Christchurch Harbour and tuckered out a bit to sea, not very far, just enough to get a good view. The completion that Stefano and Paul experienced on Studland Beach together in physical union, they, Andy and George, had on their boat in a serene, cerebral, perhaps even spiritual way: they sat next to each other, close, close enough to feel each other's presence, but not holding hands or intentionally touching, just so close that what was between them was nothing more than proximity. And they watched in equal awe and wonder, equal to each other, equal to that of spectators elsewhere. They did not take pictures, or videos; they sat in the little boat they had 'borrowed', bobbing up and down a bit on the shallow waves of a calm sea with a subtle breeze coming in more or less from their left now, as they were facing the beach. They knew they had done a terrible thing.

Beautiful, outrageous. Gorgeous. And terrible. With dawn now creeping home on them too, George started the engine of the little boat and drove it straight to the shore where they landed not far from Boscombe Pier. Once again, nobody really took notice of them, two pale, dishevelled teenage figures, as they wandered along the beach, absorbing the gash of a wound they had inflicted on it: hut after wrecked hut, smouldering in the morning haze. The odd fire still burning. Water puddles from where people had attempted to extinguish a blaze. Ruined belongings. Melted plastic crockery and disfigured chairs. Exploded gas bottles and broken glass. Splinters of wood, singed at the edges. Blackened, browned. And every now and then, not often, but here and there, the blue or amber flashing lights of ambulances and police. Surprisingly few fire engines. But ambulances and police. And yellow tape now, here and there, and blue and white tape too, and then, mixed into the smell of coal and sulphur and burnt wood and overheated metal, a different smell, an alien, unfamiliar one, sweet and pungent in equal measure.

Here is where George, instinctively, without noticing, took Andy's hand, and when they had been walking slowly before, they now moved with hesitation, caution, peering between the people who in places gathered, in places stood forlorn, in places comforted each other, surrounded by those now busy, answering the call of catastrophe: the rescue personnel, the life savers, the paramedics and the competent bystanders turned volunteers. A sheet-covered body. A stretcher. A woman, terror in her eyes. The quiet, undramatic unfolding of disaster aftermath.

Moving through these scenes in silence, slowly, Andy and George, holding each other's hands, began to sense that they had attained a kind of absolute: none, not one of the beach huts they passed was unscathed. All were damaged, most were destroyed. And the loss on people's faces: they were only beach huts that had gone, not homes, not schools or hospitals, not museums, temples or shrines. But for the devastation written on these expressions, it might as well have been all of those. Cherished these huts had been, loved. The few, modest possessions each had contained had meant more to their owners than treasures in a bank vault or safe. To some cynic much may have been tat, to these people—honest, unassuming people—

they had embodied memories and harboured care.

Nothing epitomised their loss more poetically than a ceramic figure of a fat beach couple, grinning ear to ear, one a bucket in one hand with a shovel sticking out of it, the other waving a little flag, both arm in arm, with their sun hats on, standing on a mound of sand with the omnipresent caption *"life's a beach"* in thick letters embossed on it: its shards lay shattered on the ground next to the burnt shelf it had fallen from, and two disembodied chubby faces now grinned stubbornly from among char-stained debris.

George and Andy walked along the beach for a while, then went up to George's flat, where his dad was out—presumably, they thought, outside somewhere, assessing the damage, talking to neighbours; they didn't mention it or ask—they went and sat on George's bed. Then George lay on his back and Andy did so too. And Andy turned over to his side and rested his head on George's shoulder. And George put his arm around him a bit, and they fell asleep.

When they woke up it was four thirty in the afternoon, they had slept uninterrupted for nearly twelve hours. George's dad sat on the sofa in front of the television, which had the news on, showing the scene no more than seventy yards from where he was sitting, only outside. George got up, used the loo, went into the kitchen, said, 'hi dad,' and poured himself a glass of water, took it back to his bedroom, where Andy now stirred. He gave him to drink from his glass, and Andy now got up too and used the loo, and then they both went into the living room and sat down on the other sofa, at a right angle to the one George's dad was sitting on, and George's dad looked at them both and said 'are you two all right?'

Andy nodded and George said, 'yes,' and
then they sat in silence and listened to a
reporter from the beach not seventy yards
from where they were sitting, only outside,
and there they remained sitting in silence
as the reporter described the spectacular
fire and confirmed that the number of
casualties so far was twelve but could rise
as there were some people missing, and
several were in hospital with severe burns,
and among the victims were two girls who
were twins, aged five, and a picture came up
showing two lovely, lively, smiling girls, aged
around five, and there was also a dog that
had died in the fires.

George's dad was shaking his head in
incomprehension and a nondescript anger,
and Andy and George sat on their sofa at a
right angle to him, and then George got up
and went back to his bedroom and lay back
down on the bed on his back again, and
Andy followed him and lay back down on

his back next to him, and this time George turned over and put his arm around Andy, and Andy turned towards him and put his arm around George, and they lay there, not really sleeping and not really waking and certainly not dreaming, their foreheads touching and their arms oddly entwined, but in a comfort all of their own, and an hour passed, or possibly two, and then the doorbell rang.

The police had no trouble getting the boys to
confess to their actions, in detail. What they
had great trouble with was understanding
them: their motives, their emotions, their
reasons; their unnerving casual calm,
even now, even now that the extent of
the damage, the depth of destruction, the
heinousness of their deed was put before
them.

The boys, in turn, seemed to understand
and simply accept that all of this was exactly
the way it was. They expressed no regret, or
if so then only when pressed on an angry
detail: the twin girls; these beautiful, lovely,
five year old girls: did they not feel sorry for
them? Yes, they said, they did. And the dog?
The cute little spaniel? And the dog too, yes.

The police were not alone in being incapable
of understanding the boys. The moment
they issued a statement confirming their
arrest, hate rose from the ground, like
the stench of poison and decay. It spread,
and quickly it turned into anger: fury against
an incomprehensible evil that the people,
the good people of Bournemouth and
Boscombe, felt had nested in their midst and
that had, as far as they could tell, nothing
whatever to do with them.

The Earnest Psychologist, who was not,
by the way, one who ever spoke to the
boys, invoked many possible causes:
disillusionment, suppressed sexuality, self-
loathing, confusion, disorientation, parental
neglect, parental overbearing, nondescript
feelings of persecution, projection,
detachment, disenfrachisement, loneliness,
boredom, *ennui.*

The words to the people who had lost their huts, let alone those who had lost a friend, a lover, a husband, a wife; a sister, a brother, a mother, a father; least of all though to those who had lost their gorgeous twins, and also not to those who had lost their little dog, to them, these words meant nothing, they were just noise. And it made these people, these good people, angrier still, and more hateful. And the hate ate into them and turned their misery into madness: a kind of madness, an uncontrollable fear and loathing.

For their first court appearance, the boys were driven in two separate vans—why the two separate vans? some people demanded to know—the short distance from their police cells to the court building, and angry, hateful crowds gathered and shouted vile words and curses at them and called for their heads, banging on speeding police vans, endangering their own lives, rather than keeping the peace.

The ugliness was pervasive: faces distorted
in pain and wrath and dismay. Loud voices,
high pitched declamations, over and over
again: 'They've ruined our lives!' 'They
should be shot!' 'These two, they belong
locked up and the keys thrown away...'

The Angry Prophet wasn't having any of it:
'Don't you see,' he berated them, 'you made
these boys and you will make more of them:
unless and until you look into yourselves
and begin to ask questions of yourselves and
what kind of people you are that you ignore
in your midst those you dislike, there will be
ones at ever-recurring junctures that will do
some unspeakable thing, just to be heard,
just to be seen, just to know they exist. Wake
up, you dull, you smug, you sleep-walking
idiots and ask why you are so punished!'

The people did not like to hear this, they
shut off his rants, if not from their ears—he

was loud!—then from their minds: he has ever berated us thus, he is the madman here, this has nothing to do with us, these kids have gone wrong.

The Sacred Sage was silent for a long long time. He feared not for his life nor for his wisdom, he feared for the humanity in these humans. After the hapless Messenger had been pushed to the ground in The Square and punched in the face and kicked in the guts and stabbed in the neck with a broken bottle and been left to bleed to death, the Sacred Sage knew: we're undone. We're undone: we need to redo ourselves.

She was just a journalist, but not of the kind that quickly make up a convenient narrative that is simple and clear and easy to understand and that puts the headline "MONSTERS" on the front page with pictures of the two young perpetrators, as others did, without hesitation; she was one who had spoken to George's crestfallen, hollowed father, to Andy's shellshocked mother, to one or two teachers and one or two friends, and who had written a piece that simply and plainly and in gentle, differentiated language, but clearly, had stated that these two boys, Andy and George, were not evil, or different, or monstrous or inhuman: they were simply two boys who had done a terrible, perhaps inexplicable thing, but that it was not unforgivable. That in fact perhaps the only way we who now grieve for the elderly couple, the twins and the dog, perhaps the only way we can now move on and make things better again is to forgive them. Soon. Not absolve them, not shrug our shoulders and say: shit happens. But forgive them. Step towards them, embrace them, comprehend them.

The people were not ready to hear this, to read it in their local paper. They let a day pass, then another, then their rage took over and they waited for her, in broad daylight: she stepped out of her office at the *Bournemouth Echo* on Richmond Hill and was making her way towards the Koh Thai Tapas on Poole Hill for a bite to eat with a friend, when they pounced on her in The Square and took her life for speaking a truth they were not ready to hear.

The Sacred Sage saw only now sorrow. But he knew then that he needed to counsel, and be his counsel never heard. He knew that his lone voice would be drowned out and that the anger, the fury, the pain and the hatred would stir these people and eat into them for a while, but if ever the anger was to surrender to wisdom, the fury abate toward knowledge, the pain ease into power, and the hatred reveal itself to be love, then he would, sooner or later, have to counsel, and this would be hard and seem futile but it was all he could do, and it was at the same time everything that he must.

And he spake thus to anyone who would listen, though nobody would:

'You are these boys, and they are you. Every fibre, every molecule, every thought, every heartbeat, every quantum particle that they are is you. You have not made them, you *are* them. You are them as much as you are the lovely twins and the cute little dog and the beautiful elderly couple. Own this part of you. And then heal it. Heal it not by hating it or attempting to expunge it, heal it by accepting that you are capable of this. You are capable of building these huts and putting into them quaint souvenirs and enjoying them with your lover, your neighbour, your friend, your gorgeous five-year-old twins and your grandparents who have been together for sixty years and who have never done or said anything vile in their lives, and you are capable of blowing them up and burning them down. You and these boys are one. I and you, we are one. I am no wiser, no sager than you. I am you too. The Messenger, whom you destroyed: she is you. All is one. We are this. This is who and what we are. We are Boscombe Beach, we are Bournemouth Town, we are the country, the world and the universe. We are God. And we are Andy and George. And Andy and George therefore, too, are God. Everything we do and everything we do not do and everything we say and everything we do not say and everything we think and everything we do not think is who we are. And since we are God, it is for us and for us alone and for us together to make ourselves Divine.'

And having spoken thus, the Sacred Sage, unheeded, stood, bare but for his simple robes, forlorn, and smiled. He smiled because he knew, being sacred, and sage, that no matter how angry, how furious, how pained and how hateful these humans were now, they were also still God, and their godliness would one day—perhaps far into an unfathomable future not yet envisaged, unknown to us yet and deep as the reach of the Thought of God itself—come true. For surely, but surely, it is so.

II

Revival

The Bournemouth & Boscombe Nude
Beach Stroll is a joyous event that happens
each year on the last Sunday in June. It starts
at midday and goes on all afternoon, often
into the evening, though not normally much
beyond sunset.

Anyone can participate irrespective of age,
gender, ethnicity, religion, sexual, affective
or otherwise expressed orientation, looks,
or outlook: it's really just an opportunity
for anyone who wants to to wander along
the beach in the buff and feel good about
it, about themselves, about each other and
about the universe.

Since nobody organises it, nobody 'owns'
it, other than the people who happen to be
there taking part in it, and since nobody
'owns' it other than in the sense that

everybody who takes part in it does, there are no rules, beyond those of common sense and kindness. What you wear or don't wear is in fact up to you, but sunscreen is generally recommended. That said, The Bournemouth & Boscombe Nude Beach Stroll takes place in any weather at all, and it is not unheard of for everybody to get perfectly drenched, effectively taking a half-day long shower, naked in the summer rain.

Many people, especially the hardier ones who cover the whole stretch from Sandbanks to East Cliff, like to don some comfortable footwear; and hats, owing to their pervasive usefulness, really come into their own here. They also come in all shapes and sizes: something of a niche subculture thrives, whereby participants with time on their hands go to town over creating their own, but this is by no means compulsory. You don't even have to wear a hat. You don't have to wear anything, that's the beauty of

The Bournemouth & Boscombe Nude Beach Stroll.

Since carrying anything, including your phone and money, is such a pain when you wear nothing, there is hardly any trade or commercial activity that particularly caters to the nude strollers. Instead, a convention has evolved whereby the hundreds of beach hut owners—whether they themselves feel compelled to join in the general nudity or prefer to wear their usual beach attire, entirely as is their wont—provide cups of tea, coffee, biscuits, or, if they are of a particularly generous bent, glasses of Pimm's to the strollers who stop by for a natter.

"There are," after all, and as many a pub and cafe along many a coastline has written on a sign above the bar or on a chalk board by the entrance, quoting Yeats, "no strangers: only friends you haven't yet met." And indeed, lifelong friendships have formed here among people who have lived maybe three or four streets away from each other, but who have never found an opportunity to as much as say hello, until they stood on the beach by another near-neighbour's hut, sipping from a mug or a disposable cup and maybe dunking a biscuit or enjoying a vape or an old-fashioned fag, overlooking the rhythmic roll of the sea.

Some of these friendships flourish into love, and quite a few of the toddlers who run along on the pebbles here probably owe their presence to this fine, and, at the end of the day, very British tradition. In that same tradition, though, sex in public is frowned upon. That is not to say, of course, that after hours and after dark, in some of the huts, or over the water at Studland, behind some of the dunes, in the relative privacy of the midsummer moonshine, some love is not made in the old-fashioned way; but in the main, and certainly for as long as the sun sits anywhere in the sky, the day and the evening are fully family friendly.

Nobody really knows now how it all started, but legend has it that two guys in their twenties had entered a dare: to streak from the Jazz Cafe at the Sandbanks end of the bay all the way—some seven or eight miles— along the sea front to the Beach House on the Christchurch Harbour.

It was about lunch time, and they reckoned the sun was most definitely over the yard arm, so they had themselves a couple of cocktails for courage, stripped naked and started to run. It took them all of about fifty yards before they were out of breath, and they thought that, while it is perfectly acceptable for mad dogs and Englishmen to go out in the midday sun, it was simply not the done thing to run. Instead, they eased into a gentle canter and then a trot, which readily transmuted into their stroll.

Strolling, they realised to their delight, had
the immense advantage of allowing them
to hold a conversation while progressing
slowly but pleasurably along the beach,
and of course their barefaced, bare-chested
cheek and unclothed loins attracted a certain
degree of attention. Also opprobrium,
at first, it has to be said, but they were
charming about it and talked to anyone who
wanted to talk to them, answering offence
with banter, and aggression with wit, and
before long some mates and then some mates
of theirs and some girlfriends and then some
girl friends of theirs and then people who
didn't really know anyone but thought they
were amongst a congenial bunch, started to
join them, and by the time they all got to
the Beach House they were having a regular
blast.

Of course, the most committed of purists
now follow the route in its fullness in the

original direction, but there is absolutely no obligation to do so: if you prefer to stroll with the sun in your eyes and head east to west, that's just as enjoyable, and if you simply want to sit on the beach or wander up and down a bit between the piers, that's perfectly fine.

The whole point, as anyone who knows The Bournemouth & Boscombe Nude Beach Stroll will tell you, is to be comfortable in your skin and to celebrate your communion with your fellow humans, without stress or strain or pressure.

I grow interested in the myth. More than
interested, intrigued. Why is it a myth?
Clearly there must be some foundation
to it. But nobody knows. Does nobody
want to know? Everybody wants to know
everything, always; but do they really?
Is it kinder on the mind, and warmer on
the heart, not to be certain, about certain
things?

Who, I wonder, were these 'two guys in
their twenties'? Shouldn't there be a plaque
to them? Should they not be celebrated as
local legends in their own, quite literally,
lunchtime? (It was around then, after all,
that they stepped, in the nude, into leisurely
'action'.) Do they still take part now, many
years later, perhaps in their thirties, or even
forties? They could be dads, by now; in
fact, if—as in any respect other than their

initiation of this curious custom they appear to be—they are fairly average males then all likelihood suggests that they are, by now, also dads.

Do they live in Bournemouth, still, or Boscombe? Did they ever? That may be a clue: perhaps they weren't actually from here. Maybe they were just visiting, this is a distinct possibility. Because if they were native to the Bournemouth and Boscombe community then surely, but surely, somebody would know who they are. Then again, if, as has been suggested, some 'mates' joined them on their first stroll, then there must have been mates to do so. Maybe they were visiting too? Perhaps they were part of a group, of an Australian sports team? Maybe a language school? They could have been hearty Scandinavians, here to learn English! Or maybe they actually didn't have any mates here at all, maybe they were just talking to strangers at first, but

became readily friendly with them, and these
erstwhile strangers who were now effectively
friends had mates and they joined them,
impromptu, and that's how it all happened.
Who knows. Well, exactly: who actually
knows?

My early investigation into this matter of
waxing importance—waxing, in importance,
at any rate, to me—yields nothing. Yes, the
Bournemouth & Boscombe Nude Beach
Stroll happens each year on the last Sunday
in June; yes, it attracts a fair bit of attention
nowadays: people come here from all
over the region, even the country, maybe
the world, but there is no website and no
guide. No official history, and no reference
to its founders. No club and no charitable
foundation. More than intrigued now, I'm
fascinated: how do these things come about?

My mind latches onto something, but
it doesn't know what. Maybe it's my

subconscious mind: it knows, it wants, it needs there to be more to this than meets the eye (though what meets the eye would, on occasion, seem to be quite enough...) and it thinks it knows that there usually is: so likelihood would suggest. And in the absence of certainty, likelihood is our friend. I want to go with that, that notion, that thought.

My mind senses, below reasoning, above intuition, that there is a connection and that this connection can be found. But not by 'traditional' means. (What, in any case, are 'traditional' means?) It realises, my mind, now, that it has to let go and take an approach that is not a route, that is not direct, that is not determinate or determined, that is neither logical nor pure, neither chaotic nor abstract, neither instinctive nor wise. So what is it? Perhaps I am overthinking it all, but that doesn't matter: I stand on the beach looking out

to the sea and I notice the air coming
in from vaguely the right. Over there.
By the headland. Is it a headland? Is it a
beach? I like the waves, they are steady and
impermanent at the same time. They are
waves and particles too. They are full of tiny
molecules, but that is not what I mean. They
are wet but their power is implacable. If
nobody knows, then maybe they need to be
told.

I decide to delve deeper and take a detour,
via the sea. There is something somewhere
that somebody would rather were not the
case. I shall find it and let it be so...

I resolve to dive in. Not into the water—
that's way too cold for me, this time of year,
early summer, just after the solstice and
before the sea has been warmed by long days
in the sun—but into the experience of it all.

There, inside the experience, may lie a clue.
If not a clue, then perhaps an insight, a
truth. It could be random, it could be real.
My research has yielded nothing. I have
spoken to cafe owners and life guards; to
beach goers and hut holders. To dog walkers
(where they're allowed, the dogs) and to
joggers. Hoteliers, I spoke to, two of them.
And two police officers, one a young woman,
the other a young man, both attractive, both
friendly, both clueless as to the origin of this
tradition that is still, after all, fairly new; but
a tradition nonetheless. Age has no bearing
on the soul of a matter, be that a culture, a

person, a people, a place: roots burrow deep, far deeper, we know, than the living thing that we see may suggest.

Everybody, of course, has a story to tell. Most of them charming, some of them harrowing, all of them sad, in a way. I'm surprised to find that to be so. No matter whom I talk to, and for how long, there is always, always a moment of sadness. How did I miss that, in my perception, for so long? How sadness seeps through the seasons, irrespective of who you are.

Here, many remember, with a scarred sense of fondness for how it all brought them together, the Solstice Spectacle several years ago now, when two youths had set fire to almost all of the beach huts along the seafront in the most brazen, most wanton act of arson anyone could recall. Nobody refers to it now—as some 'newspapers' did at the time—as a 'massacre'; and few people, though the sadness naturally prevails, are weighed down now by sorrow over the girls, the twins, who'd perished, aged five, having been put to bed in one of the larger huts, while the parents were sharing a rare moment of intimacy, just outside, in the twinkling night of summery stars.

So into each other, so absorbed by their bodies, the parents had been at that time, that they didn't notice the bangs, or the heat, or the flames from the beach in the distance at first, or the smoke: they took them for fireworks in the sky, for being at one with each other for the first time in ages; and the chain lit up so quickly, by the time the Calor gas bottle exploded and they'd rushed back to their hut, just a few yards, a few steps really, no more, it was way too late.

The devastation still registers in the young mother's eyes; the young father holding her hands, as they sit, outside their new hut,

overlooking the sea. They are no longer
young now, these two, but they do have a son
and a daughter, aged twelve and fourteen.
They are not happy, but they're content.
And they have no anger now in their hearts,
and no hate. Then, they did, they tell me,
they wanted them dead, the two youths who
had done this to them, who had taken their
daughters. Now? Now they feel a kind of
resignation, and calm. Life is like that.

'Life is like that,' the young father, no longer
young now (maybe a little young, still),
but proud of his son whom he shows me a
picture of, after he's shown me one of the
twins, and before he shows me one of his
daughter too, says: 'life goes on; has to,
really.'

The young mother, who I know, although
she doesn't tell me, feels guilty for having
left the girls in the hut while stealing, for the
first time in weeks, maybe months, a bit of

time just with her man, to enjoy, to inhale, to taste and to have him, in the freedom of the seaside air and after the long struggles for daily survival, in and out of the sun, smiles a wan smile of undying regret. She could have saved them, her eyes—though they be adorned by kind lines after all—tell me, pleading for my forgiveness. I have no gift of forgiveness for her, it has nothing whatever to do with me: I only feel love for these people, and thank them their honesty and their trust.

'Thing is, we couldn't have saved them,' her husband, squeezing her hands, so in tune he senses her anguish without needing to ask any question, tells me: 'it was just too quick. When this kind of catastrophe strikes you down you have to, if you can, just get up again. Kids die in accidents. In a car crash. If we'd been lying there with them, and had fallen asleep, we'd both be dead too?' His voice inflects a question. The doubt. The 'catastrophe'. It sounds a little incongruent now, but true. Maybe he wants to be sure, more sure than he is. Who can blame them. I salute them, I wander on.

I do not find any relatives of the elderly couple, or the owners, at the time, of the dog. But, 'Bournemouth & Boscombe has had its fair share of tragedy,' an old lady tells me, 'maybe more than.' She sits further down the beach, in front of her own hut, that is hidden a little, tucked away behind a bit of a bluff, and she nods at me sagely. I expect her to go on, but she doesn't. There is something in my memory that I can't recall that makes me think that I know what she's talking about, but the look she gives me suggests that the time isn't right. And so I don't ask, and she doesn't tell. Some things are best left unspoken. Yet for a while. And so I take the plunge.

The Bournemouth & Boscombe Nude Beach
Stroll. I have never been naked in public.
I'm innately shy. People don't think so, they
think I am confident, bold even. I'm not.
It's the last Sunday in June and I'm curious:
will it happen. And how? The weather is
glorious, hot: more than thirty degrees. I
shower, smear sun cream all over my body,
wear shorts and a shirt and flip-flops; the
near compulsory hat, and the shades, and
head out.

It's just gone lunch time and I expect to
be disappointed. For a while it looks like I
might be; and then, suddenly, unnoticeably
almost at first, then more and more
obviously and quite naturally, it happens.
Here a naked person, another one there. A
couple, a group, some talking, some smiling,
without exception all sunning themselves
and their bodies in the luxurious heat, they
are strolling along the beach. As I get there,
they are vastly outnumbered by clothed

people, but the clothed people don't bat an eyelid, with the exception perhaps of the odd tourist. I am on my own and I don't know how to do this now, where should I stop to undress? I feel lost, I must look it, too.

I need not fret, it turns out. A big burly man with a lot of hair on his chest and a belly protruding far over a very small penis beams at me baring the broadest of grins: 'you look just like someone who's come to stroll in the nude.' For the duration of half a thought I want to say, 'sorry? Who? Me? Oh no, don't worry about me, I'm just looking for a place to buy ice cream.' But his friend smiles at me too, and I like her for that. She's generous, kind. Their mutual friend, I assume, seems to be thinking about something, but he too gives me a nod of encouragement, and so I say: 'Yes. I am.'

'I hope you're wearing sunscreen?' the big man, who steadies my arm as I step out of my shorts, asks me, and his friend

cocks his head a little as if to comment,
not strictly endorsing, but not dismissing
either, my soft cotton trunks. I take them
off too. And the shirt, and I put them all in
a little backpack I've brought along for this
purpose, and I step back into my flip-flops
and put on my hat and say: 'thank you. My
name is Sebastian.' We shake hands and they
tell me their names and I put on my shades
and we stroll.

I imagine the woman sitting across a small
plastic table from me, wearing clothes. I
confess I have done the reverse thing before.
Of course, who hasn't? Or hasn't anyone,
ever? I don't even know. It's not something
I talk about to my friends: have you ever sat
on a tube train or on a bench in the park or
in a cafe, or stood in a pub, and imagined the
people there naked? All of them? Or even
just some of them? And taken the thought
further into their world and wondered: how
do they make love? Do they 'make love', or
do they have untrammelled, wild, passionate
sex? (Why do we have to say 'have sex?'
Why, in a language that verbs like no other,
have we not adopted 'to sex' as a verb? As
in 'how do they sex?') And with whom?
What do they look like, and sound like,
and feel like, during their sexing, and in the
shower, afterwards? What will they have for

breakfast, if anything? Who or what do they see when they cast a glance in the mirror, naked? Is it normal to ask yourself these questions? Or is it weird. What isn't 'weird'? What is?

Now, I'm sitting opposite a middle aged woman who has a certain amount of volume to her body—her breasts sag a little, her tummy folds over the patch of pubic hair that adorns her vagina, her arms wobble as she gestures, which she does a fair bit—and I wonder what does she wear, normally? She has spread towels over a half dozen plastic chairs on which we all sit. My small backpack leans against mine, and part of me feels tempted, still, to just reach down now and take out the shorts and the shirt, and put them back on. Part of me though feels relaxed. Quite remarkably so.

Her girlfriend, the woman's, is pouring tea from a pot into half-size colourful mugs which have on them motifs of beach life in England. They're handcrafted and pleasant and add to the general feeling of familiarity. There is nothing remiss with this world as I see it, it seems, and I wonder why do we call our partners, if we have them, which at this time I don't, 'boyfriend' and 'girlfriend' when they are clearly way into their forties or fifties, and what, then, is a transgendered friend. Surely not my 'transfriend'?

The 'girlfriend', who is certainly nearing her mid-forties if not in fact pushing fifty, and of a similar build to her partner/lover/ otherhalf/technically-wife-though-they-be- not-married-even-though-now-of-course- they-could-if-they-wanted-to, while pouring tea into the mini mugs that are more sturdy than dainty, but lovable all the same (a bit like the couple themselves), recounts the story of their progeny—the mugs'—and how they—the couple—got them from a friend of theirs who in turn had made them herself especially for their beach hut here, outside which we are sitting, as a present.

But my mind isn't on tea or on mugs or even on the extraordinarily large buttock that advances on me alarmingly as she bends down to pour the sixth mug. Instead, my mind briefly wanders into un- or only tangentially related territory, and I wonder can we not just call this, ourselves, the Rainbow Community. We've adopted the flag, we enjoy the concept, it's served us well, it does the job and it's friendly. LGBTTQQIAAP sounds, frankly, ridiculous. It may be inclusive, but as a word it's unpronounceable, and as an acronym preposterous. And though it list everyone anyone can currently think of, it's bound to be incomplete. There is certain to be someone out there somewhere who does not feel their gender or sexual identity adequately represented by either 'lesbian', 'gay', 'bisexual', 'transgender', 'transsexual',

'queer', 'questioning', 'intersex', 'asexual', 'ally',
or 'pansexual'. Rainbow, let's face it, does
the trick, as in: 'Brighton & Hove is a haven
for the Rainbow Community, there is no
real reason why Bournemouth & Boscombe
shouldn't be too.'

I have a feeling the idea can hardly be
new, and I surmise it has probably been
tried or at least aired before and for some
reason or other rejected, or dismissed, by
at least some. But, my mind goes: we need
better than a string of letters that looks
like an unsolved Enigma code and has no
sound. 'Rainbow' is fine, seriously. It may
have hippie connotations, and the peace
movement of the 1990s may have a claim
on it too, but so what. It's embracing. It's
non-ethnicity specific, it's even pretty. It's
natural. Rainbows happen all over the world.
All the time. Like living, like loving. Like
questioning, querying and doubting. Like

being naked under the sun. For whatever reason, to whatever end.

We could call ourselves the Turing Community, with a reference to the unsolved enigma that is being LGBTTQQIAAP, and to honour a human who has done more for humanity than most others and suffered terrible injustice as his reward. I resolve to try it out on my new friends here, at the next opportunity and say something like: 'The Turing Community has really made great strides this century, but the struggle is by no means over.' Upon which they are bound to ask: 'What's the Turing Community,' to which I'll reply: 'Us, the Rainbow Community,' and there'll no doubt be a long discussion about what we should call ourselves, and whether we can even think of ourselves in any way as a 'community'. And that could be fun, or at least diverting. Or conversationally stimulating, who knows...

Before I can do so, we are joined by another friendly couple who are participating in the Bournemouth & Boscombe Nude Beach Stroll together with their little dog. The dog is panting a bit in the heat now, so he gets a bowl of water as a priority. Everybody gets up, that is my big burly new friend, who's effectively adopted me as a Nude Beach Stroll newbie, his somewhat demur friend who has not been saying much since I tagged along with them, and their sunny woman friend whose welcome it was that had convinced me and won me over so quickly.

The British ritual of kissing friends and close-enough friends of friends, even if you have never met them before, on the cheek, once—or twice? you can never be entirely sure which—here takes on an additional layer of 'slightly awkward', because parts of peoples' bodies that are usually unnoticeable enough, wrapped in some clothing, now dangle and wriggle, and you just have to get used to the odd nipple or tip of a cock brushing against you, and make nothing of it. As do these kind folk, whom to be with I feel happier and more comfortable about all the time.

There is now a veritable plethora of people represented around this little impromptu tea party, and instead of toying with gender nomenclature, I imagine them going about their ordinary business during the day naked. That's just as entertaining, I quickly realise, as imagining them clothed. The host couple, it transpires, are both social workers of some sort, though one, it appears, in the statutory, the other in the voluntary sector. The mixed couple who have just arrived are semi-retired, it seems, but I can't quite disentangle their various community involvements and interests from their part time professional activities, which lie broadly in the region of 'consultation'.

My burly new friend is a carpenter, and his
friend who turns out to be his partner—the
one who strikes me as a little suspicious, or
possibly simply wary of me—a lawyer. Their
woman friend works for a big company
on the outskirts of town. In personnel. I
imagine being employed by her big company
on the outskirts of town and needing
to see her about my annual leave or my
P45, and wandering through a large open
plan office full of naked people sitting at
computers doing things that to me are
incomprehensible in the way, say, cricket
is, but not quite as fascinating or soothing,
and knocking on Jane's door and hearing
her friendly, warm, sunny voice call, 'come
in!' and finding her sitting there at her own
desk with her big broad smile, and her very
red lips and her quite strawberry hair and
her freckled nose and her large-nippled
breasts, and her necklace that has a Buddhist,
I reckon, symbol on it, or maybe it's just

generically spiritual, and her interesting
silver green-shade coloured nails. And I
imagine her offering me a seat.

There are many things inherently impractical
indeed about being naked. You don't want
to, for example, sit down in a leather chair
where you know someone else has just sat,
for maybe half an hour or longer, talking to
their Human Resources manager about a
recurring health issue. What exactly is the
issue, you wonder, and is it contagious?...
Or the carpenter. Now, in some respects that
makes a little more sense: making furniture
is proper physical exertion, and why should
he not do so free from textiles, but perhaps,
for reasons of personal safety, no more than
topless...

I like his chest, Paul's, as it bounces when
he laughs at a joke I wasn't quite listening
to and therefore didn't quite get, and I like
his magnificent belly which doesn't seem fat

so much as voluptuous. He is wholly, and wholesomely, attractive, though not in a classical, or traditional, or obvious way. His personality beams and bestows on the people around him reassurance. I like that. His living partner (of many years, it transpires) is the exact opposite. Dry and wry and analytical. They obviously complement each other, and although he, the boyfriend— yes, you see, it really doesn't work for him, 'boyfriend'—hasn't warmed to me yet, I sense his underlying suspicion, if that's what it is, slowly ceding. It's maybe the tea, maybe the realisation that I am not going to be a threat to him or his relationship, ever; or perhaps it's the cookies. I wonder could it possibly have happened that we've been served hash cookies, without being told, but then dismiss that idea as absurd. I would have fallen asleep by now, because my tolerance of dope is practically zero.

I suddenly long for a prosecco and wonder
is that an option, when I'm pulled out of
my disjointed but pleasurable reverie (in
the nude) by hearing my name spoken, loud
and a little provocative: 'and what is it *you*
do, Sebastian?' Clare asks me with a look
of frank expectation. She's the girlfriend
of the host couple and the one, I believe,
whose social work is more statutory. I'm
momentarily startled, and before I can
prevent myself from thinking the thought,
I wonder, but for a fraction of a second,
what happens when nudists get involuntary
erections, but I gather my senses and I reply:
'I am a writer.'

As the day draws to a close, and the sun now
lingers—mellowed by the dusky haze—over
the horizon, down vaguely to the right, for a
while, before bidding the shore goodnight,
I start feeling just a tad chilly, and I'm not
alone.

Much as there was no gong and no whistle,
no starting gun and no fanfare to announce
the beginning of the Bournemouth
& Boscombe Nude Beach Stroll this
midsummer Sunday, so there is no clarion
to call people back into their clothes, or to
summon them into the pubs and the bars,
or back to their houses, should they have
no friends, and made none during the day,
or simply show no inclination to hang out
into the evening. Instead, with the colder
air breezing in from the sea, and the rays at
their acuter angle subdued, you start to spot

a jumper here, and a cardigan there. The hats come off, for a while, as they are no longer needed for shade and not yet against wind, and the T-shirts go on, and once you're wearing a top there really is not much of an incentive not to also wear something around your wriggly rump any more. So on come the shorts, gradually, and the jeans and the chinos, without anyone making a deal of it, big or small; and by and by, the beach and the seafront, the deckchairs, the benches, the plastic seats outside the beach huts, and all the promenade, they start to look 'normal' again.

Of course, I'm bound to find myself asking, what's 'normal'? And it's not a facetious question, this, here. A Sunday talking to people—all kinds of people—strolling and pausing, stopping here for a drink, there for a tea, meeting friends of my new friends and their friends who introduced me to theirs, my frame of reference for any such thing as normality has been blown wide open, and it hadn't exactly been narrow to begin with.

There was a university lecturer from Leicester whose sister lives in the country with her husband and their three kids; they all were out and about, the kids mainly playing down by the water, the adults mainly standing around, nursing pints. There was the former MP whom I thought I recognised, but I didn't: I got her mixed up with somebody else, and from the wrong party. She was there with her boyfriend, and he had bumped into some mates who were actually kicking around a ball for a while. That was quite a sight, for, I warrant, these were not athletes... There was a bus driver and the obligatory cab driver too, and several nurses and teachers. Some middling managers of one enterprise or another, and a sizeable contingent of hipsters, in every sense of the word.

The overriding feel of the entire day was
defined by nothing so much as by its
extraordinary ordinariness. Perhaps it's
the mindset: the easing into this ease, the
deliberate nonchalance of letting it all hang
out, quite literally, and not paying attention,
to any of it. All day long. I suspect that
regular goers to nude beaches find none of
this anywhere near as noteworthy as I do;
I imagine that they've been saying so, all
along. For me, it was new. Though not, hand
on heart, entirely unexpected.

I don't know what I expected, but planted
in my mind from somewhere had been
a vision of a perfectly normal day in the
sun, with perfectly normal people doing
perfectly normal things, in the nude. And
that's just exactly what it was. More or less.
Of course, there was something of a garden
party atmosphere, with all this milling and
strolling and stopping for chats and Pimmses
and fruit bowls and the ubiquitous tea. Of

course, it was an especially leisurely day. In
an especially ordinary way.

Is nudity a great leveller? Of course it is.
Is it liberating? In some sense, no doubt.
Is it practical? Absolutely not. Do I wish
me more nude days in more towns of this
world, just like this? I'm not even sure. One
of the things that makes the Bournemouth
& Boscombe Nude Beach Stroll on the last
Sunday in June every year such a special
occasion is, perhaps, that it is, after all,
special. And it really helps being by the
seaside. Near a small town. (Or a couple
of them, to be precise.) It helps being in
England, maybe, I don't know. There is
still—after all—an unruffled no-nonsense
albeit quaintly eccentric friendliness in this
country that, with all the madness in and
around it, manages just about to keep it
sane. At least so it feels. Especially on a day
like today. Or is it all just nostalgia? Am I
hankering after a world that has changed

beyond recognition, that simply no longer exists, and projecting upon what is there my idyll, in a quirky distortion?

Not from my experience today. The people I met and spoke with today are just exactly as I've always experienced them, only more so. Maybe that's what the nudity does, more than anything: it lays us bare, of course, that's pretty obvious, but does being bare make us more vulnerable? Certainly. In every way. Does being more vulnerable make us more honest? Very possibly. Does being more honest make us better humans? I like to think so. Honesty in all cases in all circumstances in all situations? Maybe not. Maybe a civilisation needs to mask part of its face some of the time (maybe some part of it even all of the time?); maybe in order for it to be civilised in the first place, it needs to be clothed, in something or other. Skins, textiles, manners, etiquette, agreed upon forms of conduct, the compact of the exchange to make it bearable, pleasant even…

I'd been taken, all through the day, with how civil everyone was. How unirritable, how forgiving. Perhaps that's what it does to us, being naked: could it be that perhaps it encourages us, allows us, even, to forgive?

I decide that the origin is clearly not what matters. It goes against my grain somewhat to accept this, because wasn't that what got me onto this story in the first place? Wasn't that the intriguing question: how did it all begin? Still, nobody knows, and no-one I met and talked to about it was able to give me any more hints or pointers.

There's the legend of the two guys in their twenties and their dare, and there is the tradition that has established itself over time, and that's all there is to it. Does there need to be more? Of course, everything has a cause and an origin somewhere, and probably this is somehow known: in the fabric of the common consciousness, unspoken, unexplained. It just happened, we all know it just happened, we kind of understand how it happened, and we're all right with that. Or

is it a case of avoiding uncomfortable truths?
What could possibly be uncomfortable in
a truth about an event as friendly and as
inclusive and as welcoming and as joyful as
the Bournemouth & Boscombe Nude Beach
Stroll?

I decide to let it go. This obsession with clear
causes and rational effects. I've had, against
all my expectations and severe reservations,
a marvellous time in the unclothed company
of strangers who turned out very much to be
friends I hadn't yet met. This belief I've held
always, borne out by experience. We are good
people. Yes, we do terrible things—the litany
of our offences against each other, against
the planet, against the animal kingdom,
reads like a catalogue of monstrosity, and
we're never more than an inch away from
some appalling misdeed or other—and yes
our history is littered with catastrophic
failures of humanity, and yes: you watch
your news and you feel a moment closer to

despair before you've had a chance to change channels, but… take a Sunday afternoon like this in almost any town in England, or in any country, really, and, away from the agitation, unstirred by some cause or other, some issue or concern, given a set of basic parameters —that the fundamental needs be covered, that the fabric of the community be intact and healthy, that the framework that allows human beings to feel safe and appreciated be in place and not threatened by crime or corruption or despotic politics—you will find us getting on with each other, pretty much. Across generations, across creeds, across ideologies, across gender, across ethnicity, across religion, across our own little preoccupations, and large ones too, across the spectrum. It's not spectacular, and it's not difficult. It's human, it's normal. And yet, it still feels amazing.

This, I decide to hold on to. As a thought, as a hope. I know some will find me naive and deluded, I realise at this time of confrontation and conflict and unbearable regression into isolationist rhetoric, simplistic solutions and the allocation of blame, guilt and shame, it may sound almost glib to say: 'we are good people.' But think of the alternative.

Think of what it means if we decide, in the face of everything, that we are as terrible as the worst things we see? Then whatever makes whoever among us do wrong, in whatever way, will have won: we hand our worst version of ourselves victory over ourselves. Because yes, the bombing of children in war zones, the dumping of plastic by the container load in the oceans, the burning down of refugee centres, and the shooting of students at high schools: they're all done by us. People. Like you and me. That is the horrendous truth, but it's also—and that's much harder to comprehend and as difficult to accept—the reason there is hope yet. The people who do the most terrible things from which we recoil in disgust, they are not a different species. They are innocent when they are born and grow up with hopes and dreams of their own. And then things go wrong. Over time, bit by bit, through circumstances, through personal choices, through the need to survive, through the culture we're born into, through what behaviours are reinforced. Through illness. Through despair. For every person who does something destructive, violent, inhuman, cruel, there is also the person they could have become. May yet turn into, given the chance. And vice versa.

So if we give in to despair, surrender to cruelty, and accept violence and destruction as the norm, then we feed them. We give our energy to them, we make them stronger. We start to meet hatred with hatred, instead of with love. We start to build walls, instead of dismantling borders. We start to arm teachers, instead of disarming society. We crank up the tension, instead of defusing situations, we add fuel to the wildfire, instead of extinguishing it, and planting new trees.

They're simple choices, really: whichever version of ourselves we nurture will grow strong. And so I take my leave of Bournemouth & Boscombe and its famous Nude Beach Stroll, on the last Sunday in June. I salute you, good people, there, by the coast: I thank you, you've given me much food for thought and made me see my world differently. I do wish you well!

III

Redemption

I forget about Bournemouth & Boscombe and dedicate myself to other matters, other places, other subjects, other themes. The world is a wondrous sphere, I am reminded, as I travel, as I learn. As I love: I meet new people, form new connections, find myself enthralled to new ideas and smitten by new beauty. New affections, new reciprocities, new inspirations. New experiences.

Out of the blue, an email arrives in my inbox, via my website: the kind of message that comes in the shape of a contact form. I get those now and then, though rarely. Seldom enough, in fact, for me to take note and think: ah, someone has gone to the trouble of writing to me.

This one is more unusual still: it's a letter. Not a note or an enquiry, not a compliment

or a rebuke, not a proposition of a
collaboration or a proposal for a project.
As I read, my hopes and doubts coalesce
into a balm of both comfort and pain. The
pain that has been caused and that has not
been forgiven, the comfort of sensing that
forgiveness may, after all, be attained. It is
not, however, for me to forgive. I have not
been wronged. No more, at any rate, and no
less, than we all have by those who trespass
not against us personally but against our
understanding of what it is to be human, and
to be good. The two don't always go cheek
by jowl, I know, but deep down, is it not the
case that we would wish them to?

We know when our sense of justice, of
respect and compassion is offended, and the
offence this letter speaks to is a grave one,
truly, genuinely. The way this offence offends
is not the kind that we hear expressed now
so often when somebody faces an opinion
they don't like or encounters an expression

that is outdated maybe, even archaic. It
is an offence that comes from a senseless
act of destruction that ended and altered
lives which had no reason and no need and
certainly no desire to be so altered, so ended.
It is the offence of an irredeemable act of
violence, a cruel and wanton incision into a
community's whole existence.

The letter offers a kind of reconciliation. It
is written in a direct, unembellished style,
though carefully worded and a little formal.
Its authors have clearly given it thought,
and, by the looks of it, rather than simply
typing it into the online contact form,
they have composed it, edited it, spell-
checked it: it contains no trivial errors as
would be attributable to haste or lack of
concentration. It is purposely positioned to
be read and absorbed, not fired off as a quick
response. It goes like this:

Dear Sebastian

We enjoyed your piece on the Bournemouth & Boscombe Nude Beach Stroll a lot. Enough for us to feel moved to break our silence. Our silence was part self-imposed, part decreed. We felt for a long time that no-one should hear from us, ever again. The anger we caused, and the pain. The loss. We don't talk about it, ever, and we don't like to write about it either. Words seem weightless, when put into the balance of what we have done. At the time of our trial, we were very young. Some people have taken us saying so as an insult. 'You were young,' they say, 'but you knew what you were doing.' We did, and we didn't. When we say we were young, we don't mean to make an excuse for our actions. We mean to say: we had very little experience of what it is to be alive and we had very little understanding of what makes us human. We had no excuse. Nor did we have a reason. But we did something we knew at the time was deeply wrong. We knew this, we just didn't know how not to do it. That may not make much sense to you and you may wonder, what on earth does it have do with the Bournemouth & Boscombe Nude Beach Stroll?

You see, the hatred we faced and the anger that was vented against us, in words that were brutal and vicious, they shocked us. What did we expect? Praise? Obviously not. We didn't expect anything. Once what we'd done and the effect that it had had sunk in, we didn't expect any leniency or compassion. We couldn't understand ourselves, how could we expect anybody else to understand us? But perhaps— just perhaps—it is true to say that we were hoping for some form of forgiveness. And we were frightened and perplexed that that wasn't forthcoming. At all. From a society steeped in a religion that has sin and forgiveness at its core, we received no indication that this society at large was prepared to forgive us. Ever. There were some exceptions. But the general tone from the people, as far as we could hear, was a clamour for revenge. Newspaper journalists— again with some notable exceptions that you are well aware of—echoed this general people's call for us to be hanged. And damned. Or, at the very least, locked up in eternity, 'with the keys thrown away'. We were teenagers. Yes, we had taken innocent lives, including the lives of two beautiful girls. That that was not our intention is, we realise, irrelevant. We could have known, and we were old enough to appreciate, that setting fire to hundreds of beach huts with a series of small but devastating explosions would endanger people, and do so in a way that we could not control.

At our trial—it has been noted with disgust— we did not express any remorse, let alone ask for forgiveness. It is hard to explain why: did we not realise we had wronged people, and not just the ones who were directly affected, but also everyone who knew and loved them; in fact, everyone, because who would not see and not know that destroying people's property while risking their lives is wrong? Again, we don't want this to sound like an excuse. But expressing your sorrow, your remorse and contrition for something that is so obviously and so categorically wrong is almost impossible. If you accidentally make a mistake and knock into someone on the pavement or spill a drink and cause a little damage: that's easy. It's easy to say 'sorry' for a mini-misdemeanour. But for a crime against society? We didn't have the words. We didn't have them then, we barely have them now. When today we write to you to say: we are truly and profoundly sorry for what we have done, do you accept that as our apology? Maybe you do, because maybe you can, but you are just a distant bystander, an observer: a recounter of events, a narrator. What about the parents of the girls? The grown up children of the elderly couple? Those who loved and needed and cherished them? What about the owners of the dog? And what about those who nursed and attended the injured. In the end we were responsible for the deaths of two girls aged five, an elderly couple, and the little dog; and there were seventeen injured; two, we later learnt, with life-changing injuries. Can they 'accept an apology'? Ever? Even we don't see how. Even we don't see how anything we could say would ever be enough. How anything we could do would ever be enough. We are unable to atone for our crime, because the crime was so futile, so pointless, so deliberate and yet so random.

Us being unable to atone for our crime, and there being no words that we can find to say we are sorry, it took us a long time—until now— to formulate anything at all. We have lived in silence, mainly so as not to compound our offence. We'd been separated at our arrest and were kept apart for a while after sentencing. But our social workers and eventually our probation officers agreed that we were not a danger to society any longer, and we were allowed to get back together. We have been *together ever since: we live together, with our new identities that we were given to protect us from the wrath of the people, in a remote part of these isles, which of course we cannot and wouldn't wish to disclose. And we thought: perhaps there is something we can try. It was, yet again, not something we fully thought through. But at least it was harmless. And we had to break the terms of our parole, but we'd been out of prison a few years by then, and we thought, perhaps this is not going to redeem us and it certainly isn't going to make things good for those whom we'd wronged, but perhaps we can almost run this as a test. We will either be caught and found out and probably—so we felt—torn to pieces on the spot, or we will get away with it and that will be that. The world, we will then accept, has found a way to allow us to be now. We are, after all, now completely ordinary. Really. We both have jobs in our local community. Nobody knows who we are, and they like us. We are the kindly, now soon-to-be middle aged couple who shop at*

Waitrose together and go for walks. We admit it: we enjoy our lives. That alone, we also understand, will to many people be outrageous. It is unfair, unjust, even.

We have done time in prison, we have undergone many hours of therapy with our workers, we have cost the taxpayer hundreds of thousands of pounds. And we are happy. We are not light of heart or full of joy: that will never be possible. We are too conscious and too conscientious for that ever to be the case. The burden of our past and our offence will rest on our shoulders forever. But we are content. We are content that we have found a way now of being good citizens and of contributing to our community, without fuss. It is not atonement, so much, as it is a rational way of handling the day to day reality of being alive, after all. Was it worth sparing us, or would the world have turned into a better place if we'd been done away with? We can't answer that question objectively, we're too close to ourselves. But we like to think that the world is a slightly better place for having us in it, still. It can say: 'These boys, they did something unforgivable, but in a way we forgave them. We rose above their crime, we allowed them not to be defined solely by their premeditated act of cruelty. Ours is a world in which that is possible.' This, we believe, is a better world than a world that can only say: 'an eye for an eye and a tooth for a tooth, and you wronged me so I wrong you back just the same, and your right to life is forfeit because you took life: you have no chance of redemption, ever.'

So a few years ago, when we were still quite young, but no longer the juvenile delinquents of yore, we did something we thought was worth a try. We took a train to Bournemouth. We were not strictly allowed to do so: we are not now and will never be allowed to set foot on the scene of our crime, but we did so anyway, because we wanted to test the water. Not literally, but metaphorically. We wanted

to find out what the people of Bournemouth &
Boscombe were really like. We'd seen so much
of the ugly face of people's understandable
scorn and anger, hatred and pain, we had
forgotten, we felt, what being normal, human
and gracious would be. So we stripped off all
our clothes. We were going to run, at first,
because we were incredibly scared, as you
perhaps can imagine. But within minutes
we realised: these people, these good people
of Bournemouth & Boscombe: they are not
angry or hateful at heart. They were angry
and hateful because we had wounded them so.
But now, now that we laid ourselves bare and
walked along that same beach in front of those
same huts—the huts that had taken the places
of those we'd destroyed—people smiled at us.
They started talking to us. They even joined
us. They had a laugh with us, and a banter.
A pint and a stroll. All we'd really wanted
to test was whether we'd survive the people of
Bournemouth & Boscombe for half a day.

*We did not mean to start a new thing. But
here, and this is something we are today really
glad to tell you, we were met with love. People
were friendly and generous, good-humoured
and kind. That's what we will forever now
cherish and what we will take to our graves.
We are both not very religious, but we light
five candles every night: two for the girls, two
for the elderly couple, and, yes, one for the dog.
That dog was somebody's friend. It deserved
not to die at our hands. And while until a
few years ago that moment in the evening of
honouring and remembering them was mainly
filled with remorse and sorrow, since we
went on our beach stroll in Bournemouth &
Boscombe in the nude, it is filled now also with
love. The love these people gave us—those same
people whom we had so badly abused and who
had therefore so understandably hated us so—
sustains us today. We are grateful for it, and
we appreciate it. And we love you all back.*

*We take no credit for having 'invented' the
Bournemouth & Boscombe Nude Beach Stroll.
If the people of Bournemouth & Boscombe
didn't have it in them to do this every year, it
would not have caught on. The fact that it did
and that it now attracts visitors from all over
the world has nothing to do with us. Nobody
even knows about us. It has everything, and
only, to do with the people who make it happen
each year: the people of Bournemouth &
Boscombe. They own it, and for as long as they
want it, they may keep and enjoy it.*

*So should we even tell you about us, if we don't
matter at all? We thought long and hard
about this, and many times before we sent this
letter to you decided against it. But there was
something about your piece that convinced us,
in the end, that the truth—even though it is
painful and maybe unwelcome—still forms
part of the picture, and the picture is only
truthful if in the end, at some point, when it
is ready to be so, it can be rendered complete.*

*The colours, the layers, the light and the shade.
And so we commend this letter to you to do
with it as you see fit. But we thank you for
having prompted us now to write it.*

Yours humbly

Andrew & George

I'm struck by the fact that they're signing
it 'Andrew & George'. Was not Andy the
junior partner, drawn into the maelstrom
of cataclysm by the older, more devious
George? Maybe time has levelled their
relationship, as it levels everything, and in
all seriousness: does it matter? By sending
me their letter they have given me two
options only: to either be the keeper of their
secret, or to be the agent of their revelation.
It is a simple choice to make. I cannot be
the keeper of a secret that was volunteered
to me as a revelation. And as I believe
in redemption, and in catharsis as a step

towards it, I opt to let this stand now, here, as it is.

In my universe, hatred to love is as darkness to light: one may not exist without the other, but there is no question, ever, of which yields to which:

Love conquers all.

www.ingramcontent.com/pod-product-compliance
Lightning Source LLC
Chambersburg PA
CBHW021326060726
47591CB00006B/1882